This Little Tiger book belongs to:

_____

_____

_____

For my lovely brothers
~ J B

LITTLE TIGER PRESS
1 The Coda Centre, 189 Munster Road,
London SW6 6AW
www.littletiger.co.uk
First published in Great Britain 2002
This edition published 2002
Text and Illustrations © 2002 Jo Brown
Jo Brown has asserted her rights to be identified
as the author and illustrator of this work under
the Copyright, Designs and Patents Act, 1988.
Printed in China • LTP/1800/1762/1216
All rights reserved • ISBN 978-1-85430-784-2
5 7 9 10 8 6

Jo Brown

Where's my Mummy?

LITTLE TIGER PRESS
London

One day, a large egg
rolled out of a nest,
down a hill, and landed
at the bottom with a
CRACK!

With a push and a shove,
a small green head popped out.
It was a baby crocodile.
"Where's my mummy?" he asked.

Little Crocodile looked around and saw a monkey hanging from a branch.

"Are you my mummy?" he asked.

"Well, can you swing from a tree like me?"
asked the monkey.

Little Crocodile couldn't
even reach the lowest branch.
"And can you do this?"
said the monkey . . .

P E EEE AAA

Little Crocodile tried,
but all that came out
of his mouth was . . . .

Snap

"No, you're definitely
not a monkey, but I'm sure
you'll find your mummy soon."
So Little Crocodile wandered off
along the path, until he met . . .

. . . an elephant splashing around in the water.

"Hello, are you my mummy?" asked Little Crocodile.

"Well, can you squirt water like me?"
asked the elephant.

Little Crocodile coughed and spluttered.

"And can you
do this?" . . .

ble u

UUUU Snap

Little Crocodile tried, but all that came out of his mouth was . . .

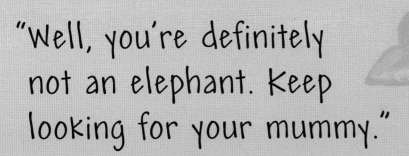

"Well, you're definitely not an elephant. Keep looking for your mummy."

So Little Crocodile wandered through the forest until he met . . .

. . . a tiger lazing in the sun.
"Hello there, are you my mummy?"
asked Little Crocodile, politely.

"Well, can you roll around in the grass like me?" asked the tiger.

"Yes!" said Little Crocodile, but he kept getting stuck . . . upside down.

"And can you do this?" asked the tiger . . . .

DOOARR

Little Crocodile tried, but all
that came out of his mouth was . . . **Snap**

The tiger definitely wasn't his mummy.

So Little Crocodile plodded
on until he came across . . .

a zebra munching some grass.

"Are you my mummy?" asked Little Crocodile, hopefully.

"Well, can you kick your back legs high up in the air like me?" replied the zebra. Little Crocodile tried but it was no use.

"And can you do this?" . . .

NAYYY HEY HEY

Little Crocodile tried,
but all that came out
of his mouth was . . . **Snap**

"No, you're definitely not a zebra,
but don't be upset. I will help you
find your mummy. Hop on my back!"

And off they went.

Before long, they
arrived at the river
where Little Crocodile
saw . . .

lots of
splashing . . .

"I think I can do that!" said Little Crocodile, smiling . . .

and he could!
"And can you do this?" asked the other crocodiles . . .

as they dived in the water with their tails in the air.

"Sure," said Little Crocodile.
"And can you do this . . . ?"

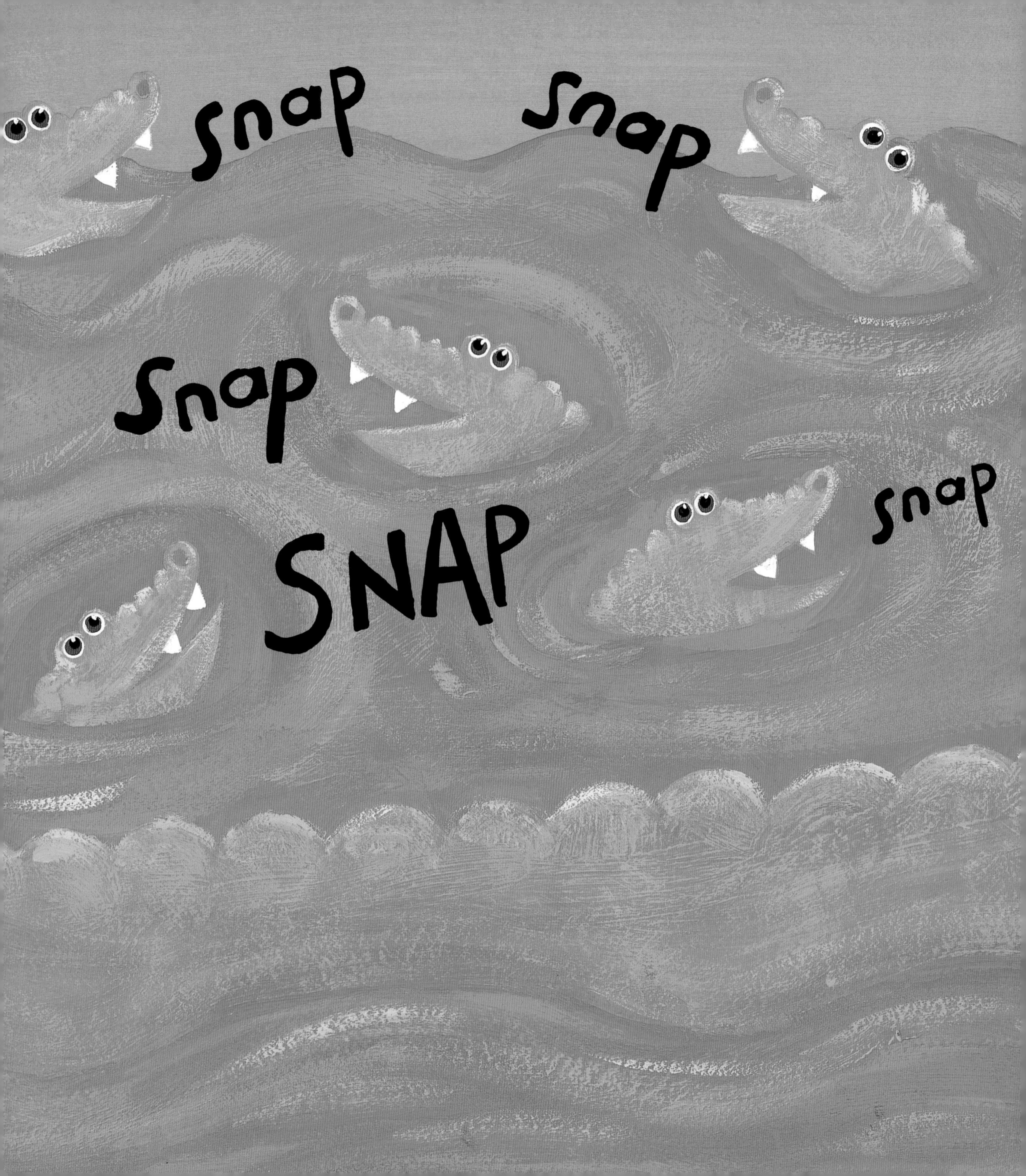
Snap
Snap
Snap
SNAP
snap

YES HE COULD!

"Oh, there you are!" said Mummy Crocodile,
"I've been looking for you everywhere."
    She gave him a big smile.
"Where have you been?"
    "Oh, just making a few friends," said
Little Crocodile.

More fabulous books
from Little Tiger Press!

I'm Special, I'm Me!
Ann Meek
Sarah Massini

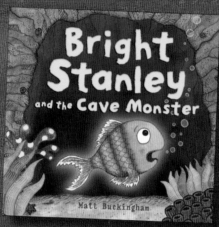

Bright Stanley and the Cave Monster
Matt Buckingham

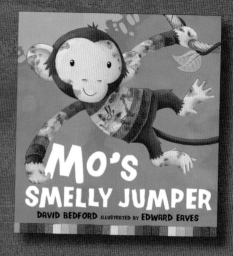

MO's SMELLY JUMPER
DAVID BEDFORD ILLUSTRATED BY EDWARD EAVES

Hoppity Skip Little Chick
Jo Brown

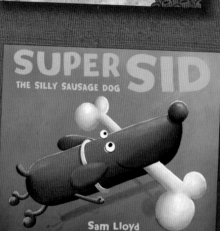

SUPER SID
THE SILLY SAUSAGE DOG
Sam Lloyd

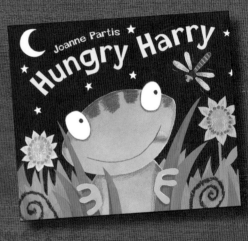

Joanne Partis
Hungry Harry

For information regarding any of the above titles
or for our catalogue, please contact us:
Little Tiger Press, 1 The Coda Centre,
189 Munster Road, London SW6 6AW
Tel: 020 7385 6333
E-mail: contact@littletiger.co.uk
www.littletiger.co.uk

Image taken from *Hoppity Skip Little Chick* copyright © Jo Brown 2005